For Cecily and Arrietty

First published 2014 by Walker Books Ltd

87 Vauxhall Walk, London SE11 5HJ

2 4 6 8 10 9 7 5 3 1

Text and illustrations © 2014 Alex Milway

The right of Alex Milway to be identified as the author and illustrator
of this work has been asserted by him in accordance with the
Copyright, Designs and Patents Act 1988

This book has been typeset in Burbank Big Regular

Printed and bound in China by South China Printing

British Library Cataloguing in Publication Data: a catalogue record
for this book is available from the British Library

ISBN 978-1-4063-4055-6

www.walker.co.uk

PIGSTICKS AND HAROLD

AND THE INCREDIBLE JOURNEY

Alex Milway

WALKER
BOOKS

Pigsticks' Assistant

Pigsticks was the last in a noble line of pigs. His ancestors had done great things, but Pigsticks hadn't done anything yet. As he sat in his study, reading about his forepigs, Pigsticks made a momentous decision.

"Like Colonel Pigslet, I shall travel to the Ends of the Earth," he said.

But unlike Colonel Pigslet, I'll make it back alive!

EMMELINE PIGHURST

COLONEL PIGSLET

But I'll have to carry my own gear...

and I'll have to cook...

I'll need
an assistant!

Pigsticks placed an advert in the most popular

shop in Tuptown.

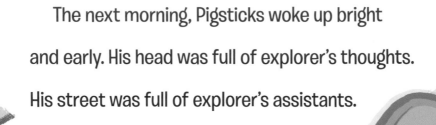

The next morning, Pigsticks woke up bright and early. His head was full of explorer's thoughts. His street was full of explorer's assistants.

EUPHEMIA PIG

INVENTOR OF THE
TROTTER PICK

LIVED HERE
1876-79

**PIRATE
GEORGE**

BOBBINS
THE ANGRY MOUSE

EVIE BIRD

Almost everyone in Tuptown had come for an interview. Pigsticks had expected as much.

"Thank you all for coming," he said. "As you know, there can be only one assistant. Therefore, the interview will be hard, but fair."

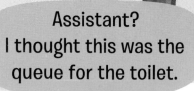

LE JEUNE COCHON AU CHANDAIL
BY FERNAND PIGGER

FISH PIG (EXTINCT)

PIGOPTRYX

SEATED PIG BY PIGASSO

THE SQUEAL
BY PIGVARD MUNCH

PIGODON
DISCOVERED
BY PIGARD OWENS

Pigsticks asked questions all morning. By the end of it, he wondered if anyone had actually read his advert.

He swallowed hard, puffed out his chest, and awarded the job to the only suitable candidate: himself.

DING DONG!

Now, who could that be?

Pigsticks opened the door to find a little hamster standing on the doorstep.

"You're too late," said Pigsticks. "The position's been taken. By me."

"Sorry," said the hamster, "but are you Pigsticks Pig?"

"I am," Pigsticks replied, "and who are you?"

"I'm Harold."

"Like I said, Harold, the job's gone," said Pigsticks.

"Oh," said Harold. "But I have a parcel for you."

I'm very busy.

"So you're not here for the job?" asked Pigsticks.

"I don't know anything about a job," said Harold, holding out the parcel.

"You're very strong," said Pigsticks.

"Thank you," said Harold, "but this parcel ... it was delivered to the wrong address."

"Honest, too," said Pigsticks. "I like that in a hamster."

Pigsticks took the parcel – it was so heavy, he nearly dropped it on his trotters.

He knew exactly what was inside.

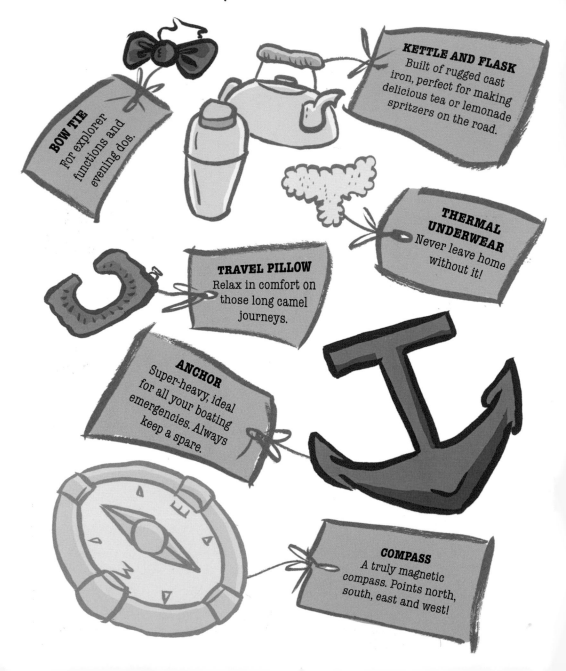

BOW TIE
For explorer functions and evening dos.

KETTLE AND FLASK
Built of rugged cast iron, perfect for making delicious tea or lemonade spritzers on the road.

THERMAL UNDERWEAR
Never leave home without it!

TRAVEL PILLOW
Relax in comfort on those long camel journeys.

ANCHOR
Super-heavy, ideal for all your boating emergencies. Always keep a spare.

COMPASS
A truly magnetic compass. Points north, south, east and west!

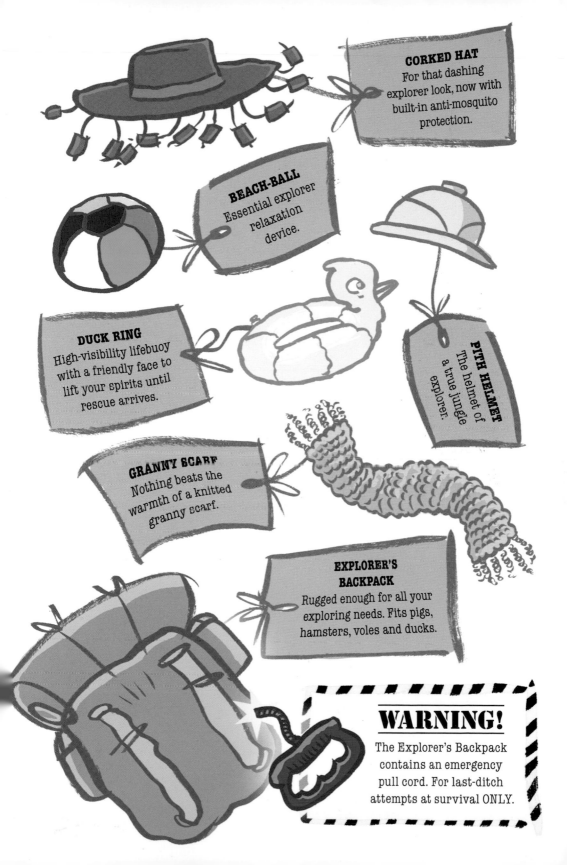

CORKED HAT
For that dashing explorer look, now with built-in anti-mosquito protection.

BEACH-BALL
Essential explorer relaxation device.

DUCK RING
High-visibility lifebuoy with a friendly face to lift your spirits until rescue arrives.

PITH HELMET
The helmet of a true jungle explorer.

GRANNY SCARF
Nothing beats the warmth of a knitted granny scarf.

EXPLORER'S BACKPACK
Rugged enough for all your exploring needs. Fits pigs, hamsters, voles and ducks.

WARNING!
The Explorer's Backpack contains an emergency pull cord. For last-ditch attempts at survival ONLY.

Pigsticks wrestled Harold into the rucksack.

It was a perfect fit.

"Have you ever been to the jungle?" asked Pigsticks.

"Not that I remember," said Harold.

"How about the desert?"

asked Pigsticks.

"I went to the beach once,"

said Harold.

Those were the words that Pigsticks wanted to hear. Harold really was an explorer's assistant.

"The job's yours," he said. "We shall leave tomorrow, before breakfast!"

"We?" said Harold.

"Yes," replied Pigsticks.

"But I'm going to a tea party tomorrow," said Harold. "There will be cake."

"We shall take a cake with us," said Pigsticks.

Harold was unconvinced. "I don't mean to be rude," he said, "but I could never leave before breakfast."

"We shall take two cakes with us!" announced Pigsticks.

"Where are you going on this adventure?" asked Harold.

"To the Ends of the Earth!" said Pigsticks.

Harold didn't know

where that was.

"And it would be just us?" he asked.

"A marvellous team!" cried Pigsticks.

Harold thought long and hard, and he eventually agreed with himself that Pigsticks was very persuasive.

"Three cakes, and I'm in," said Harold. "And make sure one of them's a Battenburg."

"It's a deal!" said Pigsticks.

He was certain that there couldn't be a more wonderful assistant than Harold.

The Long Trek

"**B**eing an explorer's assistant is hard work," said Harold.

"Being an explorer is even harder!" said Pigsticks.

Harold wasn't convinced.

He hadn't realized the Ends of the Earth would be

so far away. The march from Tuptown had been long

and difficult, and he was forced to eat one of his

cakes just to keep going.

Harold was surprised, and not a little

disappointed, when they came to a dense jungle.

"Are jungles dangerous?" asked Harold.

"Not for adventurers like us!"

said Pigsticks.

"And the Ends of the Earth are on the other side?" asked Harold.

"Exactly!" said Pigsticks.

Knowing this made Harold feel much better. They marched through the jungle for hour after hour.

"This is wonderful!" said Pigsticks. "I can hardly breathe for all the fun I'm having!"

Harold was also struggling to breathe, but he wasn't having quite so much fun.

"Only Colonel Pigslet has ever gone deeper into the jungle," said Pigsticks.

Harold was definitely going deeper into the jungle than any hamster had gone before.

"Are you sure these are stepping stones?" asked Harold.

Gradually, the jungle thinned, and they came to a terrifyingly deep ravine.

"Have we reached the Ends of the Earth?" asked Harold.

"I fear not," said Pigsticks, pointing to a rickety old rope bridge. "The Ends of the Earth lie that way!"

"That way doesn't look very safe," said Harold.

"Nonsense!" said Pigsticks. "Explorers like us eat up danger like it's sticky toffee pudding."

Pigsticks had picked his words wisely.

"If you put it like that," said Harold.

"I do," replied Pigsticks. "We shall cross that bridge and we shall reach the Ends of the Earth!"

"And when we do, will we eat cake?" asked Harold.

"Yes," said Pigsticks.

"A large cake?" asked Harold.

It was important to be clear about these things.

"A large lemon drizzle cake," said Pigsticks.

"All right then," said Harold.

"We're not there yet, are we?" said Harold.

"No, my dear friend," said

Pigsticks. "This is the desert!"

That was definitely not what Harold wanted to hear.

"Are deserts always so hot?" asked Harold.

"I believe so," said Pigsticks.

"Well I think it's unnecessary," said Harold.

Harold's backpack was getting heavier with each
step. The desert seemed to go on forever, and
everything looked the same.

"Are we going around in circles?" asked Harold.

"Good grief, no!" said Pigsticks.

The sun had reached the top of the sky, and the

scorching sand was unbearable.

Harold didn't feel quite right.

But when the desert ended, the Ends of the Earth seemed no closer. A giant ice-topped mountain rose up in the distance.

"You didn't mention a mountain," said Harold.

"I didn't?" said Pigsticks.

Harold scratched his ears, thinking hard. The heat really had got to him.

"Oh, maybe you did…" he said.

"I thought as much!" said Pigsticks. "And when we reach the top, we will eat the Battenburg cake to celebrate."

With a spring in his step, Pigsticks marched on.

"Onwards, Harold!" he said. "The end is in sight!"

Pigsticks and Harold trekked up the mountain,

battling falling rocks and icy winds.

"I can see the summit," said Pigsticks.

"Just one last push!"

"Is that the Ends of the Earth?" asked Harold, his teeth chattering.

"Of course!" said Pigsticks.

Hand in hand, the intrepid explorers braved the final ascent.

But when they arrived at the summit...

"This isn't the Ends of the Earth either, is it?" asked Harold.

There was definitely some Earth left, and Harold knew it. He'd gone as far as any hamster could go.

"There it is!" said Pigsticks, pointing. "On the horizon. Not far now!"

"Go on without me," said Harold, "I can't take another step."

"Nonsense!" said Pigsticks. "A spot of Battenburg cake will put you right."

The thought of Battenburg cake did make Harold feel slightly better. But when he looked for it, he made a shocking discovery.

"GOATS!" said Harold. "Where did they come from? They've eaten all the Battenburg!"

"Ah," said Pigsticks. "So they have."

"They still look hungry," said Harold. "And they're looking right at me."

"Don't be silly," said Pigsticks. "They'd only eat you if they were really, really hungry."

"They look really, really hungry," said Harold.

Pigsticks had to admit that Harold was right – and the goats were edging closer and closer.

"I want to go home," said Harold.

"I'll get you home," said Pigsticks. "Straight after we reach the Ends of the Earth."

"But the goats!" said Harold. He was very scared now, and the goats had them surrounded.

"Don't worry," said Pigsticks. "I've got a plan."

The Ends of the Earth

"**R**un!" said Pigsticks.

Harold couldn't run. He could barely limp.

"I'm finished," he muttered.

"Never!" said Pigsticks. "Colonel Pigslet didn't make it this far. I'm not letting a few goats get in the way now."

Pigsticks stood his ground.

"Come any closer," he said, "and you'll feel the pointy end of my stick!"

The goats weren't afraid of walking sticks.

Pigsticks decided it was time for evasive

manoeuvres. He threw Harold over his shoulder and

charged through the goats and down the mountain.

The goats chased after them.

"FASTER!" said Harold.

Pigsticks was a speedy runner, but the goats

knew all the short-cuts.

They chased Pigsticks and Harold over boulders and ice sheets and out onto a rocky dead end.

"This is it!" said Harold. "There's no way out."

Pigsticks was thinking hard, but he was exhausted. Even Harold was out of breath, and he hadn't done any running. As they awaited their end, Pigsticks was startled by the noises coming from Harold's stomach.

"I knew you were hungry," he said, "but that rumbling is very loud."

"That's not my stomach," said Harold.

"What is it, then?" asked Pigsticks.

There was no escape. The goats were back in

force, looking hungrier than ever.

"They want us for lunch!" said Harold.

"I'm starting to agree with you," said Pigsticks.

"What do we do?" asked Harold.

The goats crept closer.

Pigsticks thought for a moment. He looked over

the cliff to see what was below.

There was nothing but thick, rolling cloud.

"I knew it! It's the Ends of the Earth!' cried Pigsticks. "We made it!"

Harold plucked up the courage to look down. Pigsticks was right. They really had reached the Ends of the Earth.

"I'm sorry I doubted you," said Harold.

"We all have our bad days," said Pigsticks. "But I would never have made it this far without you."

"It's a shame we'll never make it home again," said Harold.

"This isn't the end," said Pigsticks. "We're not giving up that easily!"

Harold would have happily given up that easily – but then Pigsticks remembered something.

"The emergency pull cord!" said Pigsticks.

He delved into the remains of Harold's backpack and pulled the cord.

Two wings sprouted from Harold's backpack.

"Well I never!" said Pigsticks. "We're saved!"

"How are we saved?" said Harold.

"We've got wings! We can fly!"

"Everyone knows pigs can't fly," said Harold,

"and hamsters are even worse."

72

The goats were now within biting distance.

"You've got to trust me," said Pigsticks.

"Why do I need to trust you?" said Harold.

Pigsticks grabbed Harold and leapt from the cliff.

They hurtled through thick rolling clouds.

"This is the end!" said Harold.

"But what a way to go," said Pigsticks.

"We're flying!"

Once they were through the clouds,

Pigsticks and Harold found themselves

drifting over a sight they knew very well indeed.

WHERE EVERYONE LIVES

1. ALICE ANTEATER
2. EVIE BIRD
3. SISSY PORCUPINE
4. PIRATE GEORGE
5. MILTON RHINO
6. BENJAMIN HORSE
7. OTTERLY
8. PIGSTICKS
9. BONZO
10. BOBBINS THE ANGRY MOUSE
11. HAROLD

"Is Tuptown the Ends of the Earth?" asked Harold.

"Yes, I believe it is," said Pigsticks.

What a mess!

The whole of Tuptown came out to celebrate Pigsticks' and Harold's return. Everyone wanted to know about their adventure.

"So, Pigsticks," said Milton Rhino, "are you glad to be home?"

Pigsticks didn't need to think about his answer.

"Of course!" he replied. "But we're already planning another adventure for tomorrow. Aren't we, Harold?"